KEYBOARD INTABULATIONS
OF MUSIC BY JOSQUIN DES PREZ

RECENT RESEARCHES IN THE MUSIC OF THE RENAISSANCE

James Haar and Howard Mayer Brown, general editors

A-R Editions, Inc., publishes six quarterly series—

Recent Researches in the Music of the Middle Ages and Early Renaissance,
Margaret Bent, general editor;

Recent Researches in the Music of the Renaissance,
James Haar and Howard Mayer Brown, general editors;

Recent Researches in the Music of the Baroque Era,
Robert L. Marshall, general editor;

Recent Researches in the Music of the Classical Era,
Eugene K. Wolf, general editor;

Recent Researches in the Music of the Nineteenth and Early Twentieth Centuries,
Jerald C. Graue, general editor;

Recent Researches in American Music,
H. Wiley Hitchcock, general editor—

which make public music that is being brought to light
in the course of current musicological research.

Each volume in the *Recent Researches* is devoted
to works by a single composer or to a single genre of composition,
chosen because of its potential interest to scholars and performers,
and prepared for publication according to the standards that govern
the making of all reliable historical editions.

Subscribers to this series, as well as patrons of subscribing institutions,
are invited to apply for information about the "Copyright-Sharing Policy"
of A-R Editions, Inc., under which the contents of this volume
may be reproduced free of charge for study or performance.

Correspondence should be addressed:

A-R EDITIONS, INC.
315 West Gorham Street
Madison, Wisconsin 53703

RECENT RESEARCHES IN THE MUSIC OF THE RENAISSANCE • VOLUME XXXIV

KEYBOARD INTABULATIONS OF MUSIC BY JOSQUIN DES PREZ

Edited by Thomas Warburton

A-R EDITIONS, INC. • MADISON

ISSN 0486-123X

ISBN 0-89579-125-0

Library of Congress Cataloging in Publication Data:

Deprès, Josquin, d. 1521.
    [Works, vocal. Selection; arr.]
    Keyboard intabulations of music by Josquin des Pres.

    (Recent researches in the music of Renaissance ; v. 34
ISSN 0486-123X)
    Includes bibliographical references.
    1. Organ music, Arranged.   2. Harpsichord
music, Arranged.   I. Warburton, Thomas, 1940-
II. Title.   III. Series.
M2.R2384   vol. 34   [M12]   [M38]   780'.903'1s
ISBN 0-89579-125-0   [786.8'052]   80-24342

Contents

Preface

This volume contains a selection of music by Josquin des Prez in keyboard intabulation. There are fourteen sixteenth-century sources known to include intabulations of Josquin's works, and six of these sources are represented in this edition. The works presented here have been chosen to illustrate various types of keyboard intabulation which survive from the sixteenth century. Although only a sampling of intabulations is included here, the Preface presents a general description and discussion of all fourteen sources. The section Sources of the Known Intabulations gives the location of the intabulations of Josquin's music and cites publication information for those of Josquin's original works which have been issued in modern editions. Only one of the intabulations included here has been published before.[1]

Keyboard intabulations of works by Josquin des Prez document two phenomena in music traditions of the sixteenth century. First, they reveal the process of adapting polyphonic music—originally intended to be performed by several singers or instrumentalists—to a medium for a single keyboard performer, thus demonstrating a growing awareness of the possibilities inherent in the keyboard idiom. Second, the dates of the sources for the intabulations (see below) show continued respect for Josquin during his lifetime and long after his death. The time span during which the intabulations were made covers a period from before Josquin's death in 1521 through 1583, the date of the Paix and E. N. Ammerbach Tablatures.

Sources for the present edition are the Hör, Cracow, Cabezón, E. N. Ammerbach, Kleber, and Sicher Tablatures. The other sources known to include intabulations of Josquin's music are the *Fundamentum* for Oswald Holzach; the Kotter Tablature; the Breslau 2, Breslau 6, and Coimbra manuscripts; the Lublin Tablature; and the Henestrosa and Paix prints (see list of sources for complete citations).

Of the manuscripts preserving keyboard intabulations of Josquin's compositions, only the Breslau and Coimbra collections are written entirely in score with all voices notated on staves. The other manuscripts (including those which are sources for this edition) have only the top voice notated on a staff; the lower voices are written in letter notation. The prints do not make use of staff notation at all: the Henestrosa and Cabezón sources are notated entirely in numbers, while the Paix and E. N. Ammerbach prints are entirely in letter notation.

The intabulations interpret Josquin's music either by simply recopying it with minor changes or additions, or by adding ornamentation (which is sometimes quite elaborate) to the original polyphonic lines. The intabulations in the Sicher, Hör, and E. N. Ammerbach sources are little more than faithful scores. Likewise, the Breslau and Coimbra collections add very little ornamentation in the intabulation. Tablatures by Johannes Kotter and Leonhard Kleber represent the highly ornamented style developed by the organist Paul Hofhaimer. So profuse is the embellishment in this style, that Hans Joachim Moser has called the school of organists surrounding Hofhaimer *Ornamentisten*.[2] Kotter's tablature was owned by the humanist Bonifacius Amerbach, who probably played the music privately. Kleber, on the other hand, may have played the pieces from his collection in the churches in Horb near Tübingen and Pforzheim where he was employed.[3] Despite the elaborate ornamentation in the Kotter and Kleber sources, the framework of Josquin's original is clearly recognizable. It is not clear what the origin of the keyboard tradition of the Cracow Tablature is. However, the ornamentation in this tablature is often as elaborate as that found in Kotter's and Kleber's. Cabezón's arrangements disguise the original work more than do those of his German predecessors. In many cases the profusion of the ornamental passages and figures suggests a tempo slower than that at which the piece would appropriately be sung. (All of the pieces in the present edition were probably simply adapted [intabulated] by sixteenth-century organists for their own purposes; the exact intention as to audience is not always certain—see Notes on Performance.)

Sources of the Known Intabulations of Josquin's Music

A list of each manuscript and print known to contain keyboard intabulations of Josquin's music follows. The manuscripts are listed in alphabetical order by location; the prints are listed in chronological order. For each intabulation, the foliation in the source collection is given as well as the location of Josquin's original (indicated by item number) in the complete works edition (CE) edited by Smijers.[4] An asterisk (*) indicates that a given intabulation is included in the present edition; a cross (+) indicates that it is published elsewhere. The commentary briefly outlines the significance of each source and includes information on certain especially interesting works. With each citation, the name of the tablature is given in parentheses in order to facilitate further references in the Preface.

Manuscripts

BASEL, UNIVERSITÄTSBIBLIOTHEK, MS F. VI. 26(C)
(FUNDAMENTUM FOR OSWALD HOLZACH)[5]
+ Fortuna d'un gran tempo, fol. 7v-8v (CE, Supplement 13)

This composition is attributed to Josquin only in the Kotter Tablature (see below) and in the Bologna, 1501 copy of the *Odhecaton* (fol. 80v-81r).[6] It is anonymous in Florence, Biblioteca Nazionale Centrale, MS Panciatichi 27 (fol. 106v-107r), in Paris Bibliothéque nationale, Rés. Vm⁷ 504 (III), no. 10, and in the Kleber Tablature (see below). The ornamentation in this intabulation has the same character as the intabulation of "Fortuna" in the Kotter tablature discussed below, but it is not identical. The manuscript dates from around 1515 and was probably used privately by its owner, Oswald Holzach.

BASEL, UNIVERSITÄTSBIBLIOTHEK, MS F. IX. 22
(JOHANNES KOTTER TABLATURE)
+ Fortuna d'un gran tempo, fols. 18r-19v (CE, Supplement 13)
+ Adieu mes amours, fols. 40r-41v (CE, Secular Works 35)

This collection is known as the Kotter Tablature because so much of it is written in the hand of Johannes Kotter. Kotter was a pupil of Paul Hofhaimer sometime around 1513. Hans Joachim Marx notes that Bonifacius Amerbach,[7] owner of the manuscript, added the name of Josquin to the setting of "Fortuna d'un gran tempo."[8] The setting of "Adieu mes amours" is here wrongly attributed

to Isaac. The Kotter Tablature is published in the same modern edition which contains the *fundamentum* for Oswald Holzach (see fn. 5).

BERLIN, STAATSBIBLIOTHEK, MS 40026 (LEONHARD KLEBER TABLATURE)
*Fortuna d'un grande tempo, fols. 20r-21r (CE, Supplement 13)
*Mente tota tibi supplicate, fols. 44r-47r (Fifth part of *Vultum tuum*, CE, Motets 24)
*Ave Maria, fol. 81v-85v (CE, Motets 1)

Although the elaborate intabulations in the Kleber Tablature display the influence of the school of Paul Hofhaimer, we do not know whether Kleber was actually a pupil of the famous organist. According to Hans Loewenfeld, the intabulations may be dated from between 1515 and 1524.[9] On fol. 98r, Josquin's name has been added, apparently in a hand other than Kleber's, for the composition "Inter natos mulierum." A small slip of paper left in the manuscript attributes the setting of "Ach brech die Zeyt" (fol. 2v) to Josquin. Because these attributions are so equivocal, these pieces are not listed above.

BRESLAU, STADTBIBLIOTHEK, MS 2 (BRESLAU 2)
In illo tempore stetit Jesus, no. 18 (CE, Motets 79)
Congratulamini mihi omnes,[10] no. 119

BRESLAU, STADTBIBLIOTHEK, MS 6 (BRESLAU 6)
Praeter rerum seriem, no. 2 (CE, Motets 33)
In principio erat verbum, no. 147 (CE, Motets 56)

Breslau 2 and Breslau 6 are both tablatures in score, with all notation on staves. Breslau 2 dates from 1573, and Breslau 6 is from 1567.[11] Another Breslau manuscript, Breslau 1, credits a motet, *Ave Jesu Christe rex regem* (no. 98), to Josquin;[12] however, there are no compositions in this manuscript which are unequivocally by him. Breslau 2 (no. 36) and Breslau 6 (no. 5)[13] contain versions of the so-called *Sancta Maria vel Christus resurgens*—only Breslau 2 carries an attribution of this piece to Josquin; the intabulation of the piece in Breslau 6 is highly ornamented. Kinkeldey supports Bohn's opinion that the Breslau manuscripts are conducting scores, but asserts that the pieces must also have been played at the keyboard alone.[14]

COIMBRA, BIBLIOTECA GERAL DA UNIVERSIDADE, MS 48 (COIMBRA)
Salve regina, fols. 30v-33r, (CE, Motets 48)

The music in the Coimbra manuscript is notated in score and may have served as a keyboard accompaniment for the voices (see the commentary concerning the Breslau manuscripts).[15] The Coimbra manuscript dates from the middle of the sixteenth century, June, 1559, being the only date appearing in the manuscript.

CRACOW, BIBL. CRAC. ST. SPIRITUS (CRACOW TABLATURE)—FILM FROM HARVARD UNIVERSITY, ISHAM MEMORIAL LIBRARY; DEUTSCHES MUSIKGESCHICHTLICHES ARCHIV, KASSEL, 1/1710
  *Cum Sancto Spiritu ex officio Josquini, three-voice version, pp. 19-21 (CE, Masses 16)
  Fuga Josquini, pp. 84-87
  Kyryeleyson pascale magistri Josquini, pp. 92-97
  Untitled, pp. 240-241, on p. 240, line 2: "finitur Josquin nith Ganczer"
  *Cum Sancto Spiritu ex officio Josquini, four-voice version, pp. 242-243 (CE, Masses 16)
  Fuga Josquini, pp. 324-327, 330
  Fuga Josquini, pp. 336-340

Although most of the compositions attributed to Josquin in the Cracow Tablature, which dates from the year 1548, are of doubtful authorship, the two Cum Sancto Spiritu works are intabulations of music which is definitely by Josquin.[16] Both of these pieces are intabulations of the end of the Gloria movement of Josquin's *Missa De Beata Virgine*. In the edition, the intabulation of Cum Sancto Spiritu from pp. 242-243 of the Cracow Tablature is given first because it preserves the four-voice texture of Josquin's Mass. The intabulation of the same music on pp. 19-21 of the tablature is given second because it reduces the texture of Josquin's music from four voices to three, and omissions occur at measures 7, 15, 17, 18, and 40. The other five works attributed to Josquin in the Cracow Tablature have not been determined to be authentic.

CRACOW, POLISH ACADEMY OF SCIENCES, MS 1716 (JOHANNES OF LUBLIN TABLATURE)[17]
  + Stabat mater, fol. 128v (CE, Motets 36)
  + Tribulatio et angustia, fol. 235v (CE, Motets 54)
  + Plus nulz regretz, fol. 254v (CE, Secular Works 29)

The intabulations by Johannes of Lublin are rather elaborate, and the tablature contains instruction in musical composition. This manuscript dates from the first half of the sixteenth century (i.e., from between 1537 and 1548). John White has published a complete edition of the Lublin Tablature including the works by Josquin listed above.[18]

ST. GALL, STIFTSBIBLIOTHEK, MS 530 (FRIDOLIN SICHER TABLATURE)
  *Magnificat quarti toni, fols. 42v-45r (CE, Motets 78)
  *Tribulatio et angustia, fols. 58v-59r (CE, Motets 54)
  Mente Tota, fols. 72v-73r (Fifth part of *Vultum tuum*, CE, Motets 24)
  *Virgo prudentissima, fols. 80v-81r (CE, Motets 25)
  *Victimae paschali—D'ung aultre amer, fols. 84v-85v (CE, Motets 26)
  *Adieu mes amours, fols. 90v-91r (CE, Secular Works 35)
  Ave Maria, fols. 92v-93v (CE, Motets 1)
  *Bergerette Savoyenne, fols. 122v-123r (CE, Secular Works 36)
  O admirabile commercium, fols. 129v-130r (CE, Motets 5)
  Quando natus est, fols. 130v-131r (CE, Motets 6)
  Rubum quem viderat Moyses, fol. 131v (CE, Motets 7)
  *Germinavit radix Jesse, fol. 132r (CE, Motets 8)
  *Ecce Maria genuit, fols. 132v-133r (CE, Motets 9)

According to a recent communication from Hans Joachim Marx, watermarks in the manuscript indicate that the Sicher Tablature was copied between 1516 and 1517 while Sicher studied with Johannes Buchner, himself a student of Paul Hofhaimer.[19] At the bottom of fol. 122r, Sicher wrote, "Josquini Despres O[mn]ia p[ost] posui tu mi," the meaning of which is uncertain. Osthoff has shown that the Magnificat quarti toni is definitely by Josquin despite attributions to Pierre de la Rue, Agricola, and Brumel.[20] In the present edition the chant interpolations, based on the *Antiphonale Sacrosanctae Romanae Ecclesiae Pro Diurnis Horis* (Rome, 1912), pp. 13*-16*, replace the odd-numbered versets by Josquin that Sicher had omitted from the tablature. Sicher probably played the even-numbered versets alternately with the odd-numbered verses in the chant setting.

ZURICH, ZENTRALBIBLIOTHEK, MS Z. XI. 301 (CLEMENS HÖR TABLATURE)[21]
  + *Duo: Agnus Dei II, from *Missa De Beata Virgine*, fols. 16v-17r (CE, Masses 16)
  + "Josquin," fols. 20v-21r

The Hör Tablature identifies the Agnus Dei II simply as "Duo," while the second piece in this tablature attributed to Josquin is not identified by any title here or elsewhere. Although the Agnus Dei II has already appeared in a modern edition by Marx, the piece is included in the present edition, also; this edition uses the note values just as they appear in the source, rather than augmenting them as Marx does. The Hör Tablature was compiled between the years 1535 and 1540.

Prints

LUYS VENEGAS DE HENESTROSA, LIBRA DE CIFRA NUEVA PARA TECLA HARPA Y VIHUELA, ALCALÁ DE HENARES, 1557 (Henestrosa)[22]
+ Kyrie I, from *Missa De Beata Virgine*, fol.54r (CE, Masses 16)
+ Kyrie II, from *Missa De Beata Virgine*, fol.54v, ornamented by Palero

ANTONIO DE CABEZÓN, OBRAS DE MUSICA PARA TECLA, ARPA, Y VIHUELA, MADRID, 1578 (Cabezón)[23]—copy from Library of Congress
*Agnus Dei III, from *Missa L'homme armé super voces musicales*, fol.91v (CE, Masses 1)
+ Tiento sobre Cum sancto spiritu, from *Missa De Beata Virgine*, fol.68r
*Hosanna, from *Missa L'homme armé super voces musicales*, fol.96v
*Benedictus, from *Missa L'homme armé super voces musicales*, fol.98v
*Cum Sancto Spiritu, from *Missa De Beata Virgine*, fol.103r (CE, Masses 16)
*Stabat mater, fol.105r (CE, Motet 36)
Inviolata, fol.110v (CE, Motets 42)
*Stabat mater con diferente glosa (first part only), fol.131r
Inviolata con diferente glosa (first part only), fol.134r
Benedicta es regina caelorum, fol.159r (CE, Motets 46)
Benedicta es (second version), fol.164r
+ Ave Maria (second part of Pater noster), fol.175v (CE, Motets 50)

The Agnus Dei III from *Missa L'homme armé super voces musicales* is titled "Clama ne cesses" in the Cabezón collection, referring to the canon "Cry without ceasing," indicating that the cantus firmus is virtually without rests throughout the movement. The Tiento on fol.68r is actually a work by Cabezón himself, based on motives from Josquin's Cum Sancto Spiritu. A modern edition of the Tiento is published in Charles Jacobs, ed., *The Collected Works of Antonio de Cabezón* (New York, 1972), II: 73-74. The Ave Maria is published in Santiago Kastner, ed., *Antonio de Cabezón Claviermusik* (Mainz, 1951), pp. 24-29.

ELIAS NICOLAUS AMMERBACH, ORGEL ODER INSTRUMENT TABULATURBUCH, NÜRNBERG, 1583[24] (E. N. Ammerbach)
*Cum Sancto Spiritu, from *Missa De Beata Virgine*, fol.101 (CE, Masses 16)

JAKOB PAIX, EIN SCHÖN NUTZ UNND GEBREUCHLICH ORGEL TABULATURBUCH, LAUINGEN, 1583[25] (Paix)
Veni sancte spiritus, fol.27v (CE, Motets 49)

A facsimile and partial transcription of the composition appears in J. Nicolaus Forkel, *Allgemeine Geschichte der Musik*, 2 vols. (1788-1801), 2:731-732.

Method of Transcription

In an effort to reflect the changes in notation from source to source more definitively, the notation throughout this edition shows an exact transliteration of values from the sources. Thus, we see values getting longer in the later tablatures (see fn. 1). The barlines coincide with those in each source collection; where the source shows clearly separated groups rather than barlines, barlines have been added editorially to indicate such grouping. Although Johannes Buchner, in his *fundamentum* (Basel, Universitätsbibliothek, MS F. I. 8), shows that sustained values greater than a measure in length are simply resolved by repeated pitches in the tablatures, the repetitions have been retained in the transcriptions in this edition.[26]

In the sources, each accidental applies only to the pitch before which it stands. Inflections are shown in many cases, but they are not always reliable. Inflections given in letter notation are somewhat more consistent than those on the staff, since the letter "b" indicates B-flat, while the letter "h" indicates B-natural. A curved line attached to a letter indicates inflection upward (e.g., " f " is F-natural, and " f / " is fis or F-sharp). Written entirely in letter notation, the Paix tablature has a more precise representation of the pitches. The Hör and Cabezón Tablatures are the only ones to have key signatures.

In the edition accidentals apply to the entire measure. Accidentals have been added editorially where the context seems to require them; such accidentals are enclosed in brackets.

Although each of the tablatures maintains the integrity of each line in the polyphony, the relative position of the voice parts in the score is not the same in each collection (see Table of Voice-Part Placement).

Table of Voice-Part Placement

Source	Line for Superius	Line for Altus	Line for Tenor	Line for Bassus
Kotter Holzach Kleber*	A	C	D	B
Sicher* Hör* Cracow* Lublin	A	B	C	D
Henestrosa Cabezón*	A	B	C	D
E. N. Ammerbach*	B	C	D	E

This table shows the relative position of the voice parts in each source collection which uses numbers or a combination of letters and numbers. As in the source listing on p. viii, asterisks indicate the sources used for this edition. In the table, "A" stands for the part in staff notation or the highest line of numbers; "B" stands for the first line of letters or second line of numbers; "C" stands for the second line of letters or third line of numbers; "D" stands for the third line of letters or fourth line of numbers; and "E" stands for the fourth line of letters. As in the Sicher, Hör, Cracow, and Lublin Tablatures, the Breslau and Coimbra score manuscripts and the Paix and E. N. Ammerbach prints preserve the order of voices in score as suggested by their respective ranges. The Paix print is in six voices, and the piece by Josquin in the E. N. Ammerbach print is for four.

On the top staff in this edition, the superius is indicated with stems up, the altus with stems down. On the bottom staff, the tenor is indicated with stems up and the bassus with stems down. In compositions for three voices, the upper voice is notated with stems upward on the top staff, and the lowest voice is on the lower staff with stems downward. The middle voice ranges freely between the staves. Three staves are used for five-voice compositions. Since voice parts occasionally cross their respective ranges, the transcription is made more convenient by momentarily reversing the positions; this is documented in the Critical Notes where, for example, B/C indicates that lines B and C have been exchanged in the transcription.

The Cabezón print is the only source collection to indicate time signatures. Except for pieces from the Cabezón print, all time signatures are editorial. Furthermore, whereas each pitch in all other source collections has its own rhythmic value, a single set of rhythmic values above a musical system indicates the rhythm in the Cabezón print. For each measure a rhythmic sign (¦ , ♭ , ♮ , etc.) indicates the value of the smallest of all the simultaneous notes at that point in the piece. The rhythmic values indicated by this sign prevail until a new rhythmic sign is given above the staff. The numbers indicating the pitches are then arranged in proper spatial relation to the smallest value, much in the manner of a modern score.

Notes on Performance

The music in the present edition was probably intended primarily for the organ; it may also have been played on the harpsichord. (The diminutive size of the Kotter Tablature—16 x 22.5 cm.—suggests that it would fit easily on a small keyboard desk, such as that of a harpsichord. And the title of the print of Cabezón's intabulations—"Obras de Musica para tecla, arpa y vihuela"—indicates that the music is appropriate for harp and vihuela as well as for keyboard [= tecla]; although keyboard is probably the preferred medium, since "tecla" comes first in the title.) Since all of the intabulations in this edition were made by organists (see p. vii), the sixteenth-century organ will receive the bulk of attention in the following discussion. Moreover, the preponderance of sacred music in all of the source tablature collections indicates that the organ is the most appropriate keyboard instrument for performance of these intabulations.

Small organs which sounded a single register and had a single keyboard were called *Portativ* if they could be carried and *Positiv* if they were too large to be carried. These small organs, such as the Regal (a *Portativ* with a single-reed register), were practical because the range of the keyboard did not require a great range in the length of pipes; single-labial registers, either principals or flutes, could be played on these smaller organs.

Larger organs had several registers and often had more than one keyboard for the hands as well as a pedal keyboard. These organs combined various labial registers in the massive sound of the *Blockwerk* and also contained a few separated registers. During the Renaissance these larger organs became more diverse, as ranks of pipes could be used separately from the *Blockwerk* and as new registers were invented.

In 1482 Hans Tugi had built an organ that had two divisions, each with a *Blockwerk*, for St. Peter's church in Basel. According to documents preserved from the church, Tugi arranged the instrument with two registers on each division: the *Hauptwerk* had a *Prinzipal* and a *Flötenwerk*; the *Rückpositiv* had a *Flötenwerk* and a *Zimbel*. The *Prinzipal* could be played either alone or with the *Flötenwerk*.[27]

Few organs remain in their sixteenth-century condition; builders have added registers to the original organs, or they have exchanged old pipes for new ones. However, the Dutch organ scholar Cor Kee believes that much of the original organ in the Hervormde Kerk in Oosthuyzen, The Netherlands, has survived to the present day. The date 1521, found on a piece of parchment in the organ, suggests that at least part of the instrument must survive from the early sixteenth century. The church itself had been built in 1518.[28] Thus, this organ may be considered to be an instrument representative of one of the performance media for which these intabulations may have originally been prepared. The complete disposition of the one-manual organ at Oosthuyzen is as follows:

Praestant	8'
Holpijp	8'
Quint	1⅓' (bass)
Sesquialtera	(treble)
Octaaf	4'
Mixtuur	2' V-VI
Quint	2⅔'
Octaaf	2'

In a letter to this writer, the organ builder D. A. Flentrop has provided scales for all registers of the Oosthuyzen organ, measuring the diameters of the C-pipes in millimeters. The C's are considered because scales do not change appreciably within an octave. The comparison of these measurements for the organ at Oosthuizen with similar ones in later organs reveals that these registers are of a generally narrower scale. The scales of the *Praestant* and *Octaaf* in the organ at Oosthuizen are as follows:

REGISTER	PRAESTANT (8')	OCTAAF (4')
F	84	47.5
c	67	36.5
c'	42	22
c''	27	17(15)
a''	19	10(9.5)

The *Octaaf* is a double register from a' upward, and the scale of this doubling is given in parentheses.

Like the organ at Oosthuyzen, the Choir Organ built in 1521 for the St. Laurens Church in Alkmaar, The Netherlands, was without pedal keyboard. However, in 1555 a second manual division was added as well as a trumpet register for the pedal.[29] Thus, especially when a cantus firmus line lies in the tenor range in the music of this edition, it is appropriate to play that line on the pedal. In playing the compositions contained in the present collection, the editor has found that the choice of gentle flute registers, at both eight- and four-foot pitch levels, yields an effective sound for the performance of much of the music.

The density of the texture and the frequent ornamentation in many of the intabulations suggest that a non-legato style of playing is effective in the performance of this music on the organ. One may get an idea of what kinds of ornamental figures to add by studying the intabulations of Leonhard Kleber or by reading the *fundamentum* of Johannes Buchner.[30] The symbol ⁓ in the present edition stands for the mordent, notated in the source collections by a hook below the affected note. This symbol indicates that the main note is held while the pitch below it is reiterated, as follows:[31]

Written   Edition   Played

The execution of the mordent suggests that it was appropriated by the intabulators from the idiom of stringed instruments.

The sixteenth-century players seemed to have preferred intabulating Josquin's sacred works to his secular ones, and they favored motets over Masses. The absence of intabulations of complete settings or even of complete movements of the Masses suggests that the works appearing in keyboard collections were not necessarily played in their proper liturgical position. Rather, they were played as voluntaries, perhaps for processions, during the offertory or during the communion. Indicating the extent of an organist's duties in the period, many documents attest to the possible usefulness of the music included in the present edition. For example, in 1497, Emperor Maximilian I, patron of the organist Paul Hofhaimer, commissioned Vespers music at the Nikolaus Pfarrkirche at Hall, near Innsbruck:

> And the organist will perform at all the Vesper services and at other services. In addition he will perform a daily Salve in the Chapel of our Lady. . . .[32]

In St. Gall, Abbot Gaisberg admonished the organist Negelin in 1505 as follows:

> He is not to perform at all those things which confuse the singers or positively not perform those things, whether the singers have performed them or not, of a secular nature that people sing in the streets, with the exception of motets or similar things, and the chant.[33]

As Abbot Gaisberg's notice suggests, organists may have occasionally dared to play even the secular works in the church services.

Critical Notes

In addition to citing discrepancies between the present edition and the various intabulation sources, the Critical Notes document the cases in which editorial reversal of voices has taken place, using the letters given in the Table of Voice-Part Placement on page xi. Pitches are designated in the Critical Notes in the usual way, wherein middle c is c', and the c above it is c'', and so forth.

Duo: Agnus Dei II, from *Missa De Beata Virgine* (Hör Tablature)

M. 53, lower voice, note 1 is dotted.

Cum Sancto Spiritu

a. First version from the Cracow Tablature—Mm. 1, 2, 5, 7, 11, 17, 18, and 21, only the first pitch of the four-thirty-second-note figure is notated; the rest of the figure is indicated by the symbol [symbol] , M. 35, lowest voice, final note is an eighth-note. M. 37 lowest voice, notation is unclear.

b. Second version from the Cracow Tablature— Mm. 2, 13, and 28, only the first pitch of the four-thirty-second-note figure is notated; the rest of the figure is indicated by the symbol [symbol]. M. 36, only the first pitch of the four-sixteenth-note figure is notated; the rest of the figure is indicated by the symbol [symbol] . M. 41, see entry for mm. 2, 13, and 28, above.

c. Version from the Cabezón Tablature—Mm. 34-43, positions of voices reversed, B/C.

Hosanna, from *Missa L'homme armé* (Cabezón Tablature)

Mm. 2-4 and 6-7, position of voices reversed, B/C. Mm. 32-48, 56-63, 84-93, and 98-100, position of voices reversed, B/C. M. 88, a fermata is placed over the upper stave chord in the source to mark a significant cadence.

Agnus Dei III, from *Missa L'homme armé* (Cabezón Tablature)

Mm. 13-36, stems of the two upper parts are reversed, A/B. Mm. 47-52 (first half), the stems of the inner parts are reversed, B/C. Mm. 62-68, 149-166, 178-180, and 184-233, stems of the two upper parts are reversed, A/B.

Ave Maria (Kleber Tablature)

Mm. 21-25, 28, 36-42, position of voices reversed, D/C. M. 42, altus voice, note 2 is an octave lower (g). M. 47, tenor voice, final note is a quarter-note. M. 48, tenor voice, note 1 is an eighth-note, and note 2 is a quarter-note. Mm. 49-52 and 72-76, position of voices reversed, D/C. M. 91, bassus voice, note 2 is dotted. M. 92, tenor voice, note 4 is omitted. Mm. 100-101, 103-105, 107, 114-118, 122-126, 132-133, and 138-141, positions of voices reversed, D/C.

Mente tota tibi supplicate, from *Vultum tuum* (Kleber Tablature)

M. 87, superius voice, note 1 is f'; bassus voice, note 1 is g. M. 90, both voices, notes 2 and 3 are quarter-notes. M. 99, superius voice notated a third lower throughout the m. M. 101, superius voice, note 3 is b'-flat. M. 102, tenor voice, note 3 is d'.

Magnificat quarti toni (Sicher Tablature)

ET EXULTAVIT—M. 1, superius voice, rhythm is quarter-note (a'), quarter-note (a'). Mm. 1-5, position of voices reversed, B/C. M. 2, superius voice, rhythm is quarter-note (g'), quarter-note (g'). M. 9, bassus voice, note is g. M. 10, bassus voice, rhythm is half-note (a). M. 11, bassus voice, rhythm is 2 quarter-notes (a, a). M. 12, bassus voice, quarter-note (a), quarter-note (d). Mm. 22-24, bassus voice written an octave lower in these mm. M. 46, altus voice, note is d'; tenor voice, note is b. M. 47, altus voice, note 2 is e'; tenor voice, note 1 is a. M. 48, tenor voice, rhythm is quarter-note (a), quarter-note (e).

QUIA FECIT MIHI—Mm. 11-second half of 20, 29-31, 33-34, position of voices reversed, B/C. M. 34, superius omitted; tenor, quarter-note (a), quarter-note (g). M. 35, tenor omitted.

FECIT POTENTIAM—Mm. 41 (second half)-42, position of voices reversed, B/C.

ESURIENTES—Mm. 5, 8-9, 13-14, and 19-40, position of voices reversed, B/C.

SICUT LOCUTUS —Mm. 5-6, 19-23, 27-28, 35, and 42-45, position of voices reversed, B/C.

SICUT ERAT—M. 20, position of voices reversed, B/C.

Virgo prudentissima (Sicher Tablature)

Mm. 50-70, position of voices reversed, B/C. M. 63, superius voice, source has an additional, unnecessary quarter-note (f').

Germinavit radix Jesse (Sicher Tablature)

Mm. 26-30, 36-37, 47-50, 52-55, 58, and 63, position of voices reversed, B/C.

Ecce Maria genuit (Sicher Tablature)

Mm. 11-14, 26-30, 36-40, and 63-65, position of voices reversed, B/C.

Victimae paschali (Sicher Tablature)

Mm. 7-9, 20, 24-30, 40-42 (first half), 45-46, 59-70, 74-76, 79-80, 82-84, position of voices reversed, B/C.

M. 93, bassus voice, note 3 is G. Mm. 92-96 and 103-107, position of voices reversed, B/C.

Stabat mater

a. First version, Secunda Pars, from the Cabezón Tablature—M. 150, superius voice, notes 3-6 are eighth-notes. M. 156, notes 1-4 are eighth-notes. M. 157, all parts, no rhythm indicated.

Adieu mes amours (Sicher Tablature)

Mm. 18 and 25-27, position of voices reversed, B/C. M. 30, superius voice, penultimate note is b'-natural. Mm. 35-38 and 56-57, position of voices reversed, B/C.

Bergerette Savoyenne (Sicher Tablature)

Mm. 13-15, position of voices reversed, B/C. M. 17, superius voice, note 1 is b'-natural. M. 20, soprano voice, the rest in this m. is a sixteenth-rest. Mm. 19-21, 41, and 44-45, position of voices reversed, B/C. M. 48, altus voice, eighth-rest omitted. Mm. 48-50, position of voices reversed, B/C.

Acknowledgments

The author feels indebted to his colleague James Pruett for the initial support and encouragement of this project. He is also grateful to his colleague Margaret Lospinuso who played the pieces and made helpful suggestions about the edition.

Thomas Warburton
University of North Carolina
August 1980   Chapel Hill

Notes

1. The Agnus Dei II from the *Missa De Beata Virgine* has appeared in another modern edition. See Hans Joachim Marx, *Die Orgeltabulatur des Clemens Hör, Schweizerische Musikdenkmäler*, Vol. VII (Basel, 1970). The Agnus Dei II is offered in the present edtion as the only duo to be intabulated for keyboard, and the notational format here uses the note values exactly as they appear in the source rather than augmented as in Marx's edition. For example, while Marx transcribes the tablature minim (♩) as a half-note, the present edition transcribes the minim as a quarter-note.

2. Hans Joachim Moser, *Paul Hofhaimer* (Hildesheim, 1966), p. 103.

3. A summary of Kleber's musical life is given in Hans Loewenfeld, *Leonhard Kleber und sein Orgeltabulaturbuch* (Hilversum, 1968), pp. 31-42.

4. *Josquin des Prés: Werken*, ed. A. Smijers and M. Antonowycz (Leipzig, 1925-   ).

5. A complete edition of this manuscript may be found in Hans Joachim Marx, *Die Tabulaturen aus dem Besitz des Basler Humanisten Bonifacius Amerbach* (Basel, 1967), pp. 95-96. Marx's edition includes a complete edition of the Kotter Tablature as well.

6. Helen Hewitt, ed., *Harmonice Musices Odhecaton A* (Cambridge, 1946), pp. 7-8, 375-376.

7. Wilhelm Merian, "Bonifacius Amerbach und Hans Kotter," *Basler Zeitschrift für Geschichte und Altertumskunde* (1917) XVI: 140-206.

8. Marx, *Die Tabulaturen*, pp. 16-17, 121.

9. Hans Loewenfeld, *Leonhard Kleber und sein Orgeltabulaturbuch* (Berlin, 1897), pp. 6-36. See also Karin Kotterba, "Leonhard Kleber" (Phil. diss., Freiburg im Breisgau, 1958).

10. Helmut Osthoff, *Josquin Desprez* (Tutzing, 1965), II: 289, lists the work under "Works with Conflicting Attributions."

11. See Emil Bohn, *Die Musikalischen Handschriften des XVI. und XVII. Jahrhunderts in Breslau* (Hildesheim, 1970), pp. 7-13, 22-26.

12. Bohn, *Die Musikalischen Handschriften*, p. 4.

13. See Otto Kinkeldey, *Orgel und Klavier in der Musik des 16. Jahrhunderts* (Hildesheim, 1968), pp. 275-279 for the edition.

14. Kinkeldey, *Orgel und Klavier*, p. 191.

15. Santiago Kastner, "Los manuscritos musicales ns. 48 y 242 de la Biblioteca General de la Universidad de Coimbra," *Anuario Musical* V(1950): 78-96.

16. A complete transcription is provided in Wyatt M. Insko, "The Cracow Tablature" (Ph. D. diss., Indiana University, 1969), Vol. II. See also Zdzislaw Jachimecki, "Eine polnische Orgeltabulatur aus dem Jahre 1548," *Zeitschrift für Musikwissenschaft* II (1919-1920): 206-212.

17. John White, "The Tablature of Johannes of Lublin," *Musica Disciplina* XVII (1963): 137-162.

18. John White, ed., *Johannes of Lublin: Tablature of Keyboard Music*, 6 volumes, *Corpus of Early Keyboard Music No. 6* (American Institute of Musicology). See Vol. 3: 8-14, Vol. 3: 28-30, and vol. 4: 65-67.

19. A complete edition of Sicher's tablature is forthcoming from Bärenreiter-Verlag, edited jointly by Hans Joachim Marx and Thomas Warburton, as Vol. VIII of *Schweizerisches Musikdenkmäler*. See also Walter Robert Nef, *Der St. Galler Organist Fridolin Sicher und seine Orgeltabulatur* (Basel, 1938).

20. Osthoff, *Josquin Desprez*, II:61-64. See also Winfried Kirsch, *Die Quellen der Magnificat- und Te Deum-Vertonungen* (Tutzing, 1966), p. 309, p. 537.

21. Hans Joachim Marx, *Die Orgeltabulatur des Clemens Hör, Schweizerische Musikdenkmäler*, Vol. VII (Basel, 1970). See comments under Method of Transcription. See fn. 1 above.

22. The collection is edited in Higinio Anglès, *La Musica en la Corte de Carlos V, Monumentos de la Musica Española* (Barcelona, 1944), Vol. II. See pp. 146-148 for works by Josquin.

23. Howard Mayer Brown, *Instrumental Music Printed before 1600* (Cambridge, 1965), pp. 290-294.

24. Brown, *Instrumental Music*, pp. 313-317.

25. Brown, *Instrumental Music*, pp. 317-320.

26. Carl Paesler, "Fundamentbuch von Hans von Constanz," *Vierteljahrschrift für Musikwissenschaft* V (1889): 35, quotes the principle of repeated pitches in tablatures.

27. Rudolf Quoika, *Vom Blockwerk zur Registerorgel* (Kassel, 1966), p. 22.

28. Cor Kee, "Het orgel in de Ned.-Hervormde Kerk te Oosthuyzen," *Tijdschrift der Vereeniging voor Nederlandse Muziekgeschiedenis* XIV (1935): 35.

29. A. Bouman, *Nederland Orgelland* (Leiden, 1964), pp. 42-43.

30. See Paesler, "Fundamentbuch." See also Thomas Warburton, "Fridolin Sicher's Tablature: A Guide to Keyboard Performance of Vocal Music" (Ph. D. diss., University of Michigan, 1969), Chapter VI: Ornamentation.

31. Paesler, "Fundamentbuch," p. 33.

32. Franz Waldner, *Nachrichten über die Musikpflege am Hofe zu Innsbruck* (Leipzig, 1897), p. 29. "Und der Organist zu allen derselben Vespern Amtern unnd andern Gottsdienst auf der Orgel schlagen soll. Darumb und insonderheit auch zu Pesserung des gestiften täglichen Salve in unser liben Frauen Capelle. . . ."

33. Quoted in W. R. Nef, *Der St. Galler Organist Fridolin Sicher und seine Orgeltabulatur* (Bern, 1938), p. 146. "Er sol och dehains wegs weder wenig oder vil schlachen die wil man singt noch die senger vexieren oder das final, so sy singend oder gesungen hand, zaigen sy züchend uff oder ab und dehain weltlich lied das mann uff der gassen singen schlachen sonder mütteten stuck oder der glichen und das choral."

Plate I. *Cum Sancto Spiritu ex officio Josquini*, from the Cracow Tablature, p. 21 (end of composition). (Courtesy, Isham Memorial Library, Harvard University)

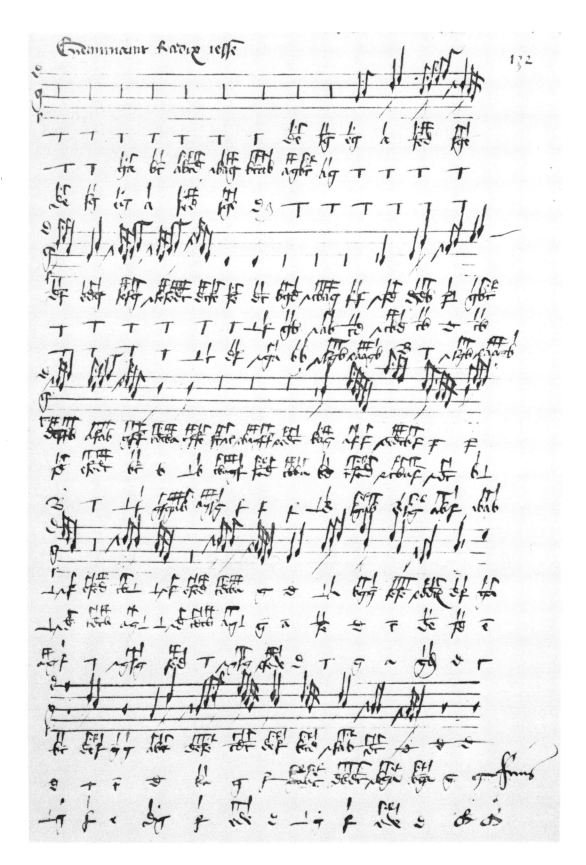

Plate II. *Germinavit radix Jesse*, from the Sicher Tablature, fol. 132r.
(Courtesy, St. Gall, Stiftsbibliothek)

KEYBOARD INTABULATIONS
OF MUSIC BY JOSQUIN DES PREZ

Duo: Agnus Dei II

From *Missa De Beata Virgine*

Cum Sancto Spiritu
From *Missa De Beata Virgine*

a. Four-voice version from the Cracow Tablature.

b. Three-voice version from the Cracow Tablature.

6

c. From the Cabezón Tablature.

d. From the E. N. Ammerbach Tablature.

Hosanna

From *Missa L'homme armé super voces musicales*

From the Cabezón Tablature.

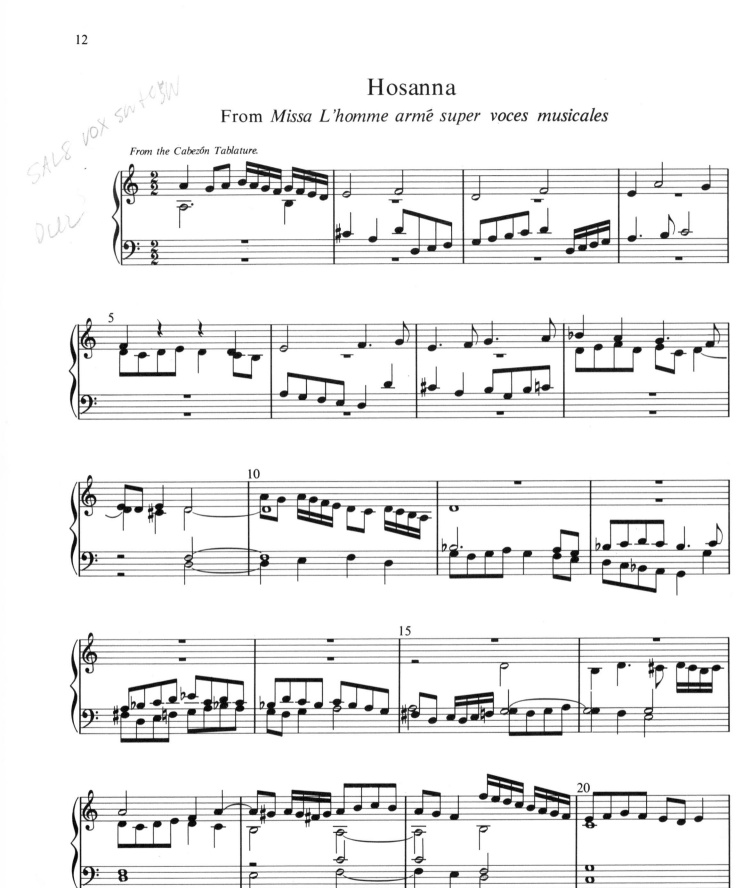

Benedictus

From *Missa L'homme armé super voces musicales*

From the Cabezón Tablature.

Agnus Dei III
From *Missa L'homme armé super voces musicales*

From the Cabezón Tablature.

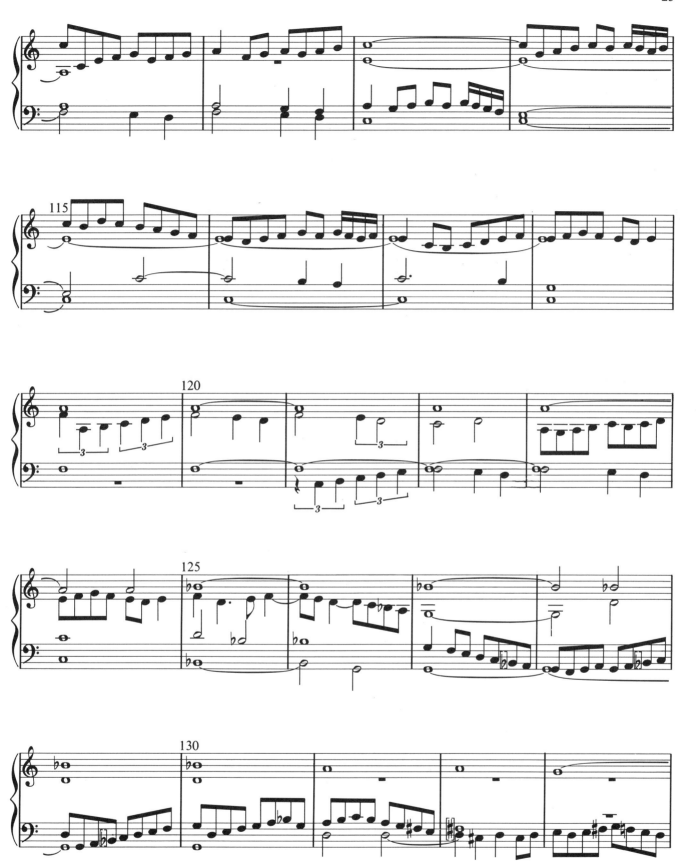

Ave Maria

From the Kleber Tablature.

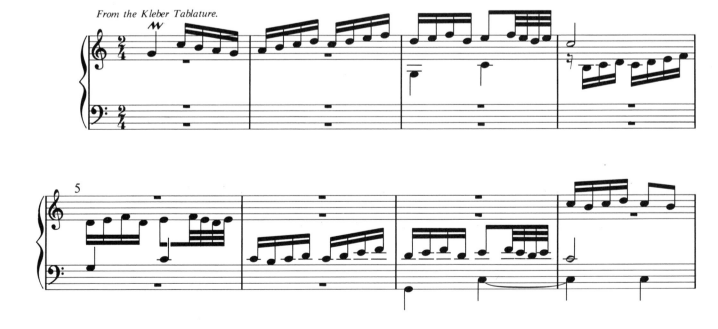

Mente tota tibi supplicate

From *Vultum tuum*

Magnificat quarti toni

*Chant interpolations from *Antiphonale Sacrosanctae Romanae Ecclesiae Pro Diurnis Horis* (Rome, 1912), pp. 13*-16*.

Qui – a re – spex – it hu – mi – li – ta – tem an – cil – lae su – ae

ec – ce e – nim ex hoc be – a – tam me di – cent om – nes ge – ne – ra – ti – o – nes.

Quia fecit mihi

Et mi— se— ri— cor— di— a e— jus a pro— gen— i— e

in pro— gen— i— es, ti— men— ti— bus e— um.

45

Fecit potentiam

46

De po — su — it po — ten — tes de se — de

et ex — al — ta — vit hu — mi — les.

Esurientes

48

Sus — ce — pit Is — ra — el pu — e — rum su — um

re — cor — da — tus mi — ser — i — cor — di — ae su — ae

Sicut locutus

Glo— ri— a pa— tri et fi— li— o
et Spi— ri— tu— i San— cto

50

Sicut erat

Virgo prudentissima

From the Sicher Tablature.

Germinavit radix Jesse

From the Sicher Tablature.

Ecce Maria genuit

Tribulatio et angustia

From the Sicher Tablature.

Victimae paschali

From the Sicher Tablature.

Pars Iª

Pars II: Sepulchri Christi

Stabat Mater

a. First version from the Cabezón Tablature.

Prima Pars

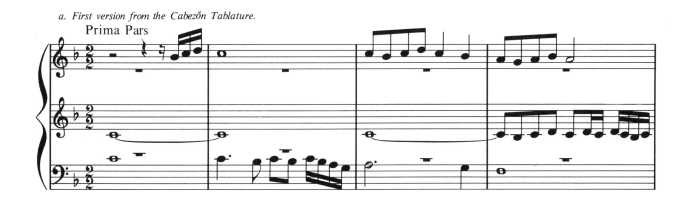

165

170

175

Secunda Pars

5

b. Second version (*Prima pars*), "con diferente glosa," from the Cabezón Tablature.

Adieu mes amours

From the Sicher Tablature.

Bergerette Savoyene

From the Sicher Tablature.

Fortuna d'un grande tempo

From the Kleber Tablature.